I0553718

Crafted Web

Bruce Martin

DEDICATION

This book is dedicated to:
My entire family
& especially to
Matthew – Never Bop Away

~ CONTENTS ~

Crafted Web

"O, what a tangled web
we weave
when we first practise
to deceive."

- *Sir Walter Scott*

1 THE TRAIN
Wednesday August 10, 1960

The express train zipped along the twin polished iron ribbons that had been stretched across the northern Illinois landscape on their bed of silver gravel and black wooden ties. Uncle Carl had died suddenly, and I was traveling to Iowa to be with my cousin, Janet. This was the second day of the rail trip, and we had just pulled out of Chicago shortly after noon. (The morning had been spent aboard the New York Central's Empire Express, and then in making connections, rushing around downtown Chicago in Checker Cabs between train stations.) We were now on the Union Pacific's Western Flyer and it was only about one o'clock. I was exhausted. Not from strenuous work, nor lack of sleep, but from the continual tedium broken only by the periods of anxiety that I associated with rail travel. It then occurred to me that earlier the New York Central's cars had been trimmed in dark gray and silver. This afternoon, on the Union Pacific, the cars had yellow with red trim.

Being brought up knowing that it was quite impolite to stare at persons (and still being somewhat shy), rather than engaging with fellow passengers, I turned my attention out the window. Not that there was much to look at. Other than the countryside filled with corn fields racing backwards toward the east, there was nothing. Occasionally though, the train would enter a long gradual curve, affording me a glimpse of its engine, some of the cars directly trailing it, and the glint of the afternoon sun reflected on the ever present track ahead. Then the train would straighten course, continue on its pace due westward, and again only the sea of corn fields would be visible.

By this point, I began focusing on minutia. Gazing through just one small area of the window, the passing corn fields began to turn, becoming an ongoing set of individual rows rather than just a passing blur. "Like the blades of an electric fan when I blink my eyes," I thought. Each row flashed in rapid succession, allowing for an instant, an unobstructed view of the open dark soil between each furrow, like when you take a deck of cards, and run your thumb across the edge, flipping the cards. But you can still make some of the cards out -- the red king, the black queen, some diamonds, hearts and spades. My mind continued to wander. What it would be like walking down one of these rows of corn, like when you're hunting pheasant in the fall, and instead of the corn being all its verdant summer green, it's just brown blades and stalks. And the ever approaching early winter wind would nudge the dead russet blades and they would make that rustling late autumn noise that only the corn knows to make. Or maybe a few weeks later I could be trudging down that same furrow, with its rich umber soil now partially frozen and mostly covered with a layer of the winter's first light snow. Still holding the stock of the shotgun, I would now be careful to avoid the stinging cold steel of the breach and barrel. I would feel and hear the crunch of the thin snowfall beneath my feet. Most the corn stalks would be gone by then, harvested for the silage. Only a few would remain scattered on the ground, interspersed among the stubble still visible on the ridges of the corduroyed furrows. Then there would be a ruffling of wings, and on one of the fence posts at the edge of the field would be a crow, cocking its head and hunching its wings as if to stay warm before being dispelled by frigid blasts to its winter's hovel. The bird would turn its head this way and that to get a better look at me. Its beady black eye, set like an onyx jewel in a crown of black feathers, would follow my every move as I progressed. I imagined that I had not seen even a solitary pheasant those two whole hours trudging along in the cold. Besides, it seemed to annoy me that the crow was perched there just looking at me. Didn't it know it was impolite to stare? I decided to speed its dismissal. Perhaps if it flew off, I could return home. I would raise my gun and fire a shot well above its beady black eye ..... I heard the loud blast of the exploding shell, and felt the sudden recoil of the gun against my shoulder. The bird and the snowy field were gone. I opened my eyes and quickly glanced at my watch.

Two thirty. Funny, I still picked up the faint acrid scent of spent gunpowder.

I settled in my seat, put my head back, staring momentarily at the ceiling, and again closed my eyes. In the blackness, the railcar's wheels made that incessant sound, colliding with each seam separating the iron rails below. Click, clack. Click, clack. Click, clack. Minute after minute. Click, clack. Then there would be an occasional crossing bell, high pitched, becoming louder, shrieking, suddenly lowering its pitch, and then fading off in the blackness. Click, clack. Click, clack. I looked down and found I was standing on a wooden plank. Below me was blackness, nothing. Click, clack. Click, clack. Slowly the plank started to move, and I was forced to walk along as it passed below my feet. Then the plank ended, and I had to step off and onto the next waiting plank. Click, clack. The space between the two planks was just a few inches, but this was absolutely terrifying as there was nothing but blackness below. But the next plank began moving gradually faster, and I had to step to yet another plank. The space to the next plank was now about a foot in length, still an easy step, I thought. Still another plank. Click, clack. And another. Click, clack. Each successive plank, though wide enough to walk along, was coming faster, and the space between them was increasing. Click, clack. I found myself running along the planks. I was no longer just stepping, but now having to bound from plank to plank. Click, clack. Click clack. Soon, I was running as fast as I could, and jumping with all my strength. Click, clack, I must jump as far as possible, and still my toes just barely reach the next plank. Nothing below. Click, clack. Click, clack. Panic was setting in. Click, clack. I felt a nudge against my shoulder. I opened my eyes.

Click, clack. "Ticket, please," the conductor asked. I found my ticket, handed it over, and he punched it – click, click. "Thank you, sir," and the conductor went on to the rows of seats ahead of me. I must have been a sight. I felt I was sweating profusely and had just run a marathon. My heart was pounding, and I was emotionally exhausted. My watch showed thirteen minutes till three. That was eastern time, as I hadn't set it back when in Chicago. I decided to stay awake until we got to our destination.

.

2 THE STATION

The train slowed. A few minutes earlier, we had crossed the Mississippi River into Iowa, and headed south. I remember thinking, "Toto, we aren't in Illinois anymore." I was relieved knowing I would be at my destination shortly, and the train would then go on through cornfield infinity without me.

The train continued to decelerate, as we entered the northern edges of the town with its factories, roadways and shops coming into view and sliding past the window. Slower now, and at last I could see the station ahead, as the train entered its curve onto the siding. We came to a crawl and stopped. The green sign at the end of the station house spelled out my long awaited destination in gold letters: JENSON. The conductor redundantly announced it: "JENSON." I got to my feet, picked up my travel case and went to the coach's forward exit.

I stepped off the train onto the platform. The station seemed remarkably similar to most other small town railway stations, with its oblong concrete platform lined with red brick, its rectangular red brick station house trimmed with green eaves, the green and gold signage, and the black iron fencing and gates separating the track platform from the street and parking areas in front of the station. There were the diamond shaped green and red Railway Express signs attached to the walls, and the green and red baggage carts left alongside the building. I turned and started walking down the platform toward the station house entrance. There was the strong but not unpleasant metallic odor of train brakes. Then the engineer released the excess air pressure from the braking system – Pffiisshhh. I noticed the men unloading the cars and I saw what I hoped was my luggage being transferred to one of the high-wheeled green baggage carts.

Upon entering the station house, my attention was immediately drawn to the massive oak railway benches that lined the room's outer edges, and were also placed back to back down the middle of the large room. I wondered -- there must be seating for at least a hundred, but there was only about seven to ten people waiting here. Following the lines of benches, the eye was drawn upward to the round clock on the far wall. Like the enormous benches in the foreground, it too was expansive. The ticket window was directly below the clock, and behind the iron bars of his counter stood the ticket master. He wore a pair of oblong octagon spectacles and atop his head was the dark blue cap with its black visor and bright red band.   He had dark mid length hair and a slightly greyed, neatly trimmed mustache. I glanced upward to the huge clock on the wall – two fifty-five.   I had forgotten to reset my watch.

*****

Glancing about, I scanned the faces in the waiting room, but other than the one or two I recognized as passengers who had just gotten off my train, I saw no one that was familiar.   Since apparently I had some time to kill, and there was more than ample room, I sat down on the empty bench facing the front entrance. I wasn't there long before the door swung open, and in walked my cousin, Janet. We recognized each other immediately, and by the time I stood up, she had rushed over and greeted me with her big, wide mid-western smile and an even bigger hug. After exchanging sincere "How are you"s, "It's so nice to see you"s, and "Gee, you're looking swell"s, I stepped back and took a good look at her. She wasn't dressed all up – just an everyday gingham top and a pair of nice blue jeans. She was still flashing that big, wide, honest smile -- the kind that says without words, "I'm really glad that you came all this way to see us, and I'm so very happy to see you!" Her whole demeanor, though I couldn't exactly describe it as bubbly, was one of an exuberant, honest, innocent, content and genuinely joyful person.   At first I thought that she was just happy to see me, but I soon saw this as a deeply rooted personality trait. It was either the result of living in a small town, or (remembering our great Aunt Dede's similar mannerisms) a trait that ran in her family. Perhaps both.   Needless to say, her personality contrasted sharply with the "normal" people I knew from the big eastern cities – people who were mistrustful, cynical, sophisticated, who could barely look you in the eye, and rarely smiled. I was glad to be in Jenson with my cousin, at least for now.

"Did you have anything to eat yet? I mean, since lunch time?" she asked.

"No," I confided, "Just some crackers at the station in Chicago."

"Well, you must be starving, then. Let's go over to the store and pick something up." (I would soon find out that she meant this quite literally.)

"What about my bags, will they be okay?"

"Sure," she replied, "of course. Nobody's going to steal them. They'll be right here when we get back. Besides, it's not like we're going to the moon or anything."

I had forgotten that the store was just across the street.

We crossed over to the Kelly Brothers General Store, which had been established, owned and operated by my two uncles, Carl Kelly (Janet's dad) and his younger brother, Dennis. The two brothers had started their business at the train station in the late thirties, selling candy and gum to the passengers, and eventually moved to the building across the street. And as they say, the rest is history. They had the ideal location, directly across from the station, and on the corner of one of the busiest routes in town.

At first blush, the storefront looked like it had been constructed with the same batch of red bricks left over from the railroad station. The store and the sidewalk were situated well above street level, so we had to really step up over the curb. The wide sidewalk, extending from the storefront to the street, was used by the proprietors to display several items for sale -- wash tubs, pitch forks, lawn mowers and other garden tools. They even had a fire truck pedal car out in front of the store.   The large windows on either side of the weathered, red-painted double door entrance were utilized for advertisement and for displaying some of the myriad items to be found inside. Perhaps most interesting was a five-foot wooden Indian, which was padlocked and chained next to the front door. (The Indian was not for sale-- some drunk once tried to run off with it.) It seemed ironic - a hundred years before, Indians were being escorted off to reservations, and now a mere replica was being chained down to keep it from being taken.

Taped to the glass on the front door was a small sign –

> *"Welcome to Kelly Brothers General Store.*
> *If you can't find what you're looking for,*
> *Just ask us.*
> *Most likely, we'll have it!!"*

This sign proved to be no exaggeration. We opened the door and bells jingled, announcing our arrival. I walked in and thought I had stepped into the pages of a Sears Roebuck catalog. There was a post card rack, key making station, deli, candy counter, displays of clothing, housewares, soda pop machines, hardware, Halloween costumes, Christmas decorations, souvenirs, tools, a grocery section, et cetera!!

Janet took a hold of my sleeve and led me down an aisle where the frozen food was kept. "How's pizza and a beer sound? Is that okay with you for dinner?"

"That's good," I replied.

So she grabbed a frozen pizza and a six pack of Pabst. "Is this okay?" she asked.

"Yeah, that'll hit the spot," I said. "Now let me pay for it."

"Nothing doing. My dad owns the store, and we don't need to pay, 'cause I work here."

(I guessed that's what she meant when she said we'd go over to the store and pick up something.)

Then I saw her face, and that smile, at the corner, started to quiver a little, and she began to tear up. "He's only been gone a couple weeks, and I miss him so already." Then she quickly regained her composure and smiled again.

"I'm really sorry about your dad." I tried to make her feel better. "He really was a nice guy."

"The best," she replied, and smiled again. "Say, what do you think you need to get for food while you're here this week?"

"Just a few things," I said. "But let me pay for them."

This time, there was no protest. I got some eggs, some coffee, bacon, bread, butter, lunchmeat, cheese and milk. She said I didn't need to worry about things like salt and pepper, and ketchup. I stopped by the magazine rack for a copy of the Chicago Tribune and an issue of LIFE – on the cover was a picture of some kids petting four or five giraffes.

We went to the counter and the helper working that afternoon rang me up. He didn't charge us for the pizza and beer.

We went back across the street to the station, put the groceries in the trunk of Janet's car (a nifty little coral and white two tone Nash Rambler Metropolitan) and went into the station house to get my bags. There they were waiting for me, just as she said --sure as shootin'.

We went back to the car, loaded up the luggage, and got in. She started up the engine. The radio had been left on and a Roy Orbison song started:

> *Dum dum dum dumdy do-wah*
> *Yay yay yay yay yeah*
> *Oh woe woe woe wah-ah-ah*
> *Only the lonely, Only the lonely.*
> *Only the lo..*

She reached over, snapped the volume control counterclockwise, and Roy was gone.

I figured I would be staying at my great Aunt Dede's house, and that's where we headed.

.

3 AUNT DEDE'S HOUSE

We drove north a few blocks, made a left turn onto Fifth Avenue South, and went on a couple more blocks. Janet stopped the car in front of a medium grey two story Victorian where our great Aunt Dede used to live. We called her great Aunt Dede, because she was our grandfather's sister (making her our great aunt) and because she really was a great and wonderful person. Her house was located on the opposite side of the street and a few doors down from the Presbyterian church, where my mom and dad were married and where we as kids used to snicker in the pews during the long sermons.

Janet helped me get the groceries and luggage out of the car, and we started toward the house. The lawn had been neatly trimmed, and flower beds adorned the front of the house on either side of the steps. A swing hung at the far right end of an open porch, and the other end of the porch curved around the corner of the house. A white wooden railing ran the length of the porch, and two large windows peered over the railing at the street, one on each side of the solid black-painted front door. We opened the door, and stepped into the foyer and hallway. I noticed an antique umbrella stand by the entrance. I set my luggage down, and helped Janet with the groceries. The hallway ran from the front door to the kitchen at the left rear of the house. Across the hallway from the kitchen was Aunt Dede's old bedroom, which remained closed. We took the groceries into the kitchen and placed them on the kitchen table and in the refrigerator. There was an entryway from the kitchen to a formal dining room at the front of the house. My cousin was showing me around the house, but most of it was still familiar as I had visited Dede a couple times before. The dining room window was one of the two windows that looked out on to the street. The house was elegantly decorated with antiques, and the dining room was no exception, boasting a large table and chairs, a china buffet, and two end tables with their art deco lamps on either side of the front window. We crossed from the dining room, back across the hall where I had left my bags, and into the parlor. I had noticed the rich dark oak flooring throughout the house, and the large rectangular floral rugs that were in the dining room and also in this room. The second of the twin windows facing the street was here in the parlor. There was an antique davenport, and a couple large bookcases filled with the complete works of such authors as Shakespeare, Poe, and Sir Arthur Conan Doyle. At the far end of the parlor was a carpeted staircase descending from the second floor, with its bannister curving gracefully into the parlor and terminating in a tight spiral. The bottom steps, in similar fashion, gently flared outward into the room.

I carried the luggage upstairs to the second floor. Near the top of the stairs, on the right side of the hallway, was an antique wind-up Victrola with a large black and gold trimmed speaker that was shaped like the inside of a morning glory blossom. There were three bedrooms and a bath that opened onto the hall from the left. It was suggested I use the second bedroom, so that's where I put my bags. Later, I would have time to further explore the second floor, and I went back downstairs to the kitchen.

*****

Janet unwrapped the frozen pizza and popped it in the oven. She mentioned that Dede had been an elementary school teacher many years ago, and that a lot of her old books and school supply items were still kept in the back bedroom upstairs. The room may also have been used as a children's playroom for the neighborhood kids and perhaps some of our other relatives. (Our great aunt had never married and therefore had no children of her own.) Janet said also there was an emergency stairway at the back of the house that led from the third bedroom (the play room) down to the kitchen. She motioned toward the door at the rear of the kitchen that opened to the back stairs. (I vaguely remembered that as a child, I was afraid to enter the back bedroom, because hanging next to the doorway to the "secret staircase," there was a picture of an old witch on her broom.)

My cousin began talking about Aunt Dede and how she used to let out the first two upstairs bedrooms to roomers, usually college aged boys who were working summertime jobs. She had asked Dede at one point if she felt safe, being an elderly woman with two men living in the house. Dede answered that she was quite okay, "but if anyone tries anything, I'll get my ball bat and flatten them."

Janet went on to say that Aunt Dede had an affinity for all kinds of elephant knick-knacks. Perhaps I had noticed some of them in the rooms- wooden carvings and brass elephants of various sizes. Dede always said, "They're spohsta bring good luck." Apparently it worked, as she had lived a happy life, without serious ailments, and had died at a ripe old age.

By this time, the pizza was done. I got two of the beers from the refrigerator, searched the kitchen drawers until I found the church key, and opened the cans. In the meantime, Janet got the pizza out from the oven and dished up a couple slices for both of us. We sat down at the kitchen table and continued the conversation.

"If you were wondering," she said, "There's all kinds of clean towels and stuff in the bathroom upstairs, and in the washroom down here off the utility area, behind the kitchen. I think you should be all set, but if there's anything you need, you can call me. I know pretty much where everything is."

"Yeah, I should be fine," I thanked her.

"By the way," she asked, "I might need some help tomorrow with some loose ends getting ready for the reception Friday afternoon. Do you think you can help me?"

"Of course, I will. Just let me know what you need me to do."

"Oh, and one other thing," she said, "You brought a suit or a sport coat and tie? I mean, I'm just checking in case if you need anything…"

"Yeah, I'm all set," I replied, "But thanks for asking."

Janet ate most of her pizza and finished about half of her beer. I, on the other hand, polished off both pizza slices and the full can of Pabst. When I asked, she said she did not want any more.

We cleared the kitchen table. I put the empty cans and scraps in the paper grocery bag to take to the trash. Janet put the dishes in the sink (I told her I'd wash them later), wrapped the leftover pizza in tin foil and put it in the refrigerator. I asked her where the trash can was kept.

"Oh, the trash can is in the back yard behind the utility room, and the garbage men come by on Tuesdays."

Since it was getting warm in the house, we decided to go out to the back yard.

*****

Janet began, "You know, my dad died from a heart attack just about two weeks ago. I guess Ophelia (his second wife) couldn't handle all the memories and the stress of him passing, so she had the cremation service right afterwards and then left on her trip to get away. Jamaica, I think."

I told her again that I was sorry about all this.

"Thank you, but I'm okay. I just wish it wasn't so sudden, since I didn't have a chance to say goodbye to him. Anyway, it was no secret that they weren't getting along so well. She started getting more and more distant, and all the while he tried to make up for it. He absolutely adored her, and tried to win her back by getting her diamonds and other fancy gifts. That didn't work, and it seemed to push her even further away. I guess after he died she felt kind of guilty and of course bad about the whole situation. She couldn't cope with it, and that's probably why she left on the long trip -- to get away from it all, I guess."

We walked around the side of the house to the front yard, and I asked her about the reception on Friday.

"Yes, the reception will be here, starting at one thirty. There's just a few people coming --the minister, a few friends and neighbors and maybe some family." She added, "Of course, my mom couldn't come, living in California and all." And then she joked, "Just don't destroy the place in the meantime."

The phrase "The wreck of the Hesperus" went through my mind. "No, I'll keep the place in tip top shape."

She thanked me again for coming all the way from New York to see her and also for offering to help her Thursday. "That reminds me, do you think you can help me out on Saturday and maybe on Monday clearing out some stuff from my dad's house? Ophelia mentioned that she wanted a lot of the stuff gone when she got back…. "

"Sure, I'll help. Be glad to," I replied. "And I want to say thanks for everything so I could stay here." It was evident that Janet had cleaned up the house, had the lawn mowed, brought in some basic supplies, and washed all the towels and bedding.

She smiled. "Don't mention it. You're more than welcome. Again, if there's anything you need, just call."

I thanked her.

She got into her car. "Bye, see you tomorrow," she said, and drove off.

*****

With the high August afternoon temperatures, and the oven going, it was still warm in the house, so I decided to open some of the windows downstairs. But with it still hot outside and with hardly any breeze, this really didn't do much to help.

I washed the dishes and put them away, then turned on the television set in the kitchen. Aunt Dede's TV was by then a few years old, so I had to wait a minute before the tubes warmed up and the picture appeared. I turned the selector knob to Channel 4, adjusted the volume, and sat down at the table. The television announcer started up, "You are watching CBS, Channel 4, WHBF Rock Island, Davenport." Then the national news programming came on the air – It was Douglas Edwards with the News: "In the news, today, U. S. Navy frogmen have found and recovered the satellite, Discoverer Thirteen. This marks the first successful retrieval of a satellite from the ocean...." My attention was diverted by the constant loud chattering of the teletype machines they had in the background. I wondered why the news programs always had them going. Did they actually serve a purpose or were they just used as a prop?

I picked up the copy of LIFE I had bought and started thumbing through it. There was some article about America's zoos and how they are helping with children's education. Then Douglas Edwards again: "In other news, Senator John F Kennedy spoke today with reporters at his summer ....." Then the TV went to an L&M Cigarette commercial with some people singing and telling me to Live Modern. Then there was a Brylcreem commercial. I had enough television for the evening. I reached over and flipped the knob to OFF, and the picture immediately collapsed into one small bright white dot in the middle of the screen. The dot gradually dimmed and then finally disappeared.

I went upstairs to the bedroom, and unpacked a few things. I took my toothbrush and other toiletries into the bath. Just as I had remembered it, there was the freestanding four-footed bathtub positioned diagonally in one corner of the room. As Janet had promised, an abundance of clean fresh towels were stacked neatly in an open cabinet. I started to go back to my room, but my curiosity got the better of me. I would take a quick look at the back bedroom just to see if it was still the same. I opened the door, and to my satisfaction, the old witch on her broomstick was still hanging on the wall, guarding the entrance to the back stairway.

*****

I had a restless night. I went to bed around ten thirty, but could not sleep. I was in a strange bed and in an unfamiliar setting, it was stifling hot upstairs, and I was still emotionally wound up from travelling. After two hours of tossing and turning, I took the top sheet off the bed and went downstairs to lie down on the sofa in the parlor. Perhaps it would be cooler on the ground floor, I thought. But still it was too warm, and sleep eluded me. I got up from the davenport and spread the sheet on the floor. I just could not sleep – the floor, though cooler, was too hard. (I was starting to feel like Goldie Locks, with everything being either too hard or too hot.) I would give the sofa one more try. I imagined the window was just beginning to lighten, and gave up trying to get to sleep. I would just wait for the dawn. I closed my eyes and rolled over.

In the blackness, I again saw the cornfields, with the crow perched atop a fence post. Then the rows of corn were flying by, and I saw the crow's jet eye peering at me from the end of each furrow. I looked again, and the rows of corn had turned to a deck of playing cards, each card flashing past me. Then, the cards began to turn, so there was only one card appearing over and over – the Queen of Spades. She was clad in crimson and black, her face drawn in a somber expression, looking slightly downward and to the side, as if posing for a portrait. Both of her soft dark eyes were visible. Then, as if seen in a kinetoscope, she gradually raised her head, cocked it sideways, and stared directly at me with one coal black eye.

I awoke with a start. The sunlight was filtering through the parlor curtains, and I needed to get ready for the day.

4 THURSDAY
August 11, 1960

I cleaned up, got dressed and went down to the kitchen to fix breakfast. I found the percolator and made a good sized pot of coffee. Other than the coffee, breakfast consisted of scrambled eggs, fried bacon, and some orange juice poured into a Fred Flintstone jelly glass (discovered in a far corner of one cupboard --Yabba-Dabba-Do!!). Once at the kitchen table, I started in with the eggs and bacon. After locating the ketchup, I inverted the bottle and smacked it on the bottom a couple times. It plopped out perfectly onto the eggs. The red ketchup on the yellow eggs reminded me of the Union Pacific color scheme. I finished up with a second cup of java.

While glancing through the Tribune, - I had left it on the table the night before - one or two items appeared interesting, but hardly noteworthy. (A precursor of the coming day, as it would turn out). I flipped over to the comic section and checked out Alley Oop and Blondie.

It was about ten after nine by the kitchen clock when the phone rang. It was Janet. She said she would be over in about an hour, if that was alright. I told her that would be fine. She said she needed to run some last minute errands, and thanked me in advance for helping her. I responded, telling her I would be happy to help out.

"Okay, thanks," she said. "I'll see you in about an hour," and she hung up the phone.

I was quite sure that whatever these last minute errands were, she could have easily handled by herself, but she probably wanted me to come along just for moral support, and to have someone there to carry things around. Anyway, she was a pleasant person, and I didn't really have much else to do. I would enjoy helping her out. Besides, she was my cousin, and she had already done so much for me.

I quickly cleaned up the kitchen, washed the dishes, made sure the parlor was straightened up, and went upstairs to make the bed and get ready.

Janet drove up in her Metropolitan coupe around quarter after ten, came up the front steps and rang the bell. I opened the door, and there she was again with that wide smile.

"How are you?" I asked politely.

"Oh, just fine, thanks."

"Do you want to come in for a minute for a cup of coffee before we leave?"

"No, that's okay, but thanks. I'd rather get started, if that's okay," she said, still beaming.

*****

We started off immediately. First, she went to some party shop to pick up some napkins, paper plates, cups, etc. After that, we went to a food store and bought some breads for sandwiches, cream cheese, swiss cheese and cheddar, crackers, mixed nuts, a jar of cherries and canned pineapple, ingredients for punch, celery and carrots.

"There," she said, "That should do it for food. Let's take this back to Dede's."

We drove back, put all the stuff away, and had a quick bite for lunch.

After that, we went to a florist to get a center piece and some other flowers, and then returned to Dede's house. Janet arranged the flowers and the centerpiece throughout the parlor and in the dining room, got the punch bowl and other party supplies ready and then turned her attention to preparing the food. She cubed the cheese and wrapped it up, prepared the cream cheese with pineapple and some with cherries, made little sandwiches (the kind without the crusts, and cut into quarters), and prepared the celery and carrot sticks. I looked on as all of this was happening, asking her periodically if there was anything I could do. Then she wrapped up the rest of the food and placed it in the refrigerator.

"Just don't get into anything," she said.

"Don't worry, I won't. But it sure looks good enough to eat," I chided.

She said she had to go home and do a few other things and thanked me for helping her. "I guess we'll be busy enough tomorrow. I'll try to get over here around ten or so to finish setting up. I'll call before I come over. See you then," she said, as she went out the door.

I watched her from the parlor window as she got into her car and drove off.

I then spent the remainder of the day relaxing and recuperating.

5 RECEPTION
Friday August 12, 1960

The guests would be arriving around one this afternoon. Janet came over about ten thirty to start setting up, and to put on the finishing touches. First, she brought in a couple pies she had made at home. She then prepared the punch and I set the bowl out on the dining table. Then she set out the rest of the food, and made sure everything was set and ready to go. Once all this was prepared, and the rooms were properly arranged, she directed her attention toward us. After we downed some leftover pizza, she turned to me and asked, "Well, do you think you need to get ready – I mean, get dressed up?" I had forgotten that I was still in my jeans and tee shirt. It was about noon, so we still had plenty of time. She mentioned that her stuff was still in the car, so while I went upstairs, she went out, got her dress clothing, and went to Aunt Dede's room to change.

I had already put my clothes out on the bed, so everything was ready. I just had to get in them. There was a pair of dark grey trousers, a black sport coat, and a freshly laundered white dress shirt with a black tie. It was one of those narrow knit polyester ties that was squared off and stitched together at the bottom. The knitted material was bulky, so I decided to use a half Windsor knot, and with some difficulty, I stuffed the tie under the rim of my collar, so it wouldn't show in back. After attaching the mandatory silver tie bar, I took one last glance in the mirror, just to make sure everything was up to par. Good enough. I closed the bedroom door and went back downstairs to the parlor.

I circled the dining room and parlor a couple times, admiring the care and precision with which the table and rooms had been arranged. After a minute or so, Janet emerged from Aunt Dede's bedroom at the end of the hallway. She was wearing a simple, yet elegant black A–line dress, with a stylish black patent leather belt and matching shoes. Light grey piping accentuated the edges of the sleeves and neckline of her dress. If I had to describe her appearance in one word, I would use "demure."

We sat down in the parlor and waited for the guests to come. It wasn't long before there was a knock at the door, and two of the ladies from the neighborhood came in. Shortly thereafter, the minister from the church on the corner arrived, immediately followed by three of our cousins (Our Uncle Dennis' children-- Denise, Dennis and Carolyn). A few minutes later, two more ladies who were friends of Janet's family came in. With hardly any exception, the guests seemed to follow the same general pattern upon arrival. They would first meet Janet, express their sympathy, and thank her for inviting them. A few of the guests brought desserts – cakes, cookies and the like – which Janet graciously accepted and placed on the dining room table. They would then either be introduced to me, or go on and mingle with the other guests already present. Of course, I was happy to speak with my other cousins, whom I hadn't seen in about seven years.

At approximately twenty minutes after one, the last guest arrived. This, I would learn, was Roberta Black. She was a rather large, heavy set woman, although I would not describe her as obese. She wore a sequined black dress, and a large black feather hat. I was busy speaking with the minister, so I couldn't describe her in detail at that point. I remember however that she seemed to be the loudest person there, and one did not have any trouble overhearing her conversation from across the room: "I know exactly, how you must feel," …. "I was so sorry to hear the dreadful news," …. "My poor dear," …. "And to think that she just up and left so soon afterwards."

I was engaged in a polite and casual conversation with the minister. He was asking where I was from and about my family. I explained to him that my mom was one of Carl Kelly's twin sisters, and that I currently lived in New York, but had grown up in Detroit. "You know, my mom and dad got married in the same Presbyterian church up at the corner, just before the… " I decided not to belabor my family history, as I saw his eyes begin to glaze over, and I did not want to seem in any way like the obnoxious woman across the room. Besides, this was a reception for my uncle and Janet. We ended our exchange on a positive note, and I told him I was very pleased to have met him.

After speaking briefly with a few other guests, I noticed that Janet was still engaged by the large woman with the black hat, so I decided to introduce myself and thereby perhaps rescue my cousin. Catching me out of the corner of her eye, Janet motioned me over -- "Jimmy, this is Roberta, one of my parents' dear neighbors."

"Hello," I said politely, yet hesitantly.

"Jimmy? Little Jimmy Franklin? Well, I don't know if you remember me, but I'm Roberta Black. My friends just call me Bertie."

The large woman with the sequined black dress was now standing directly in front of me. She was an older woman (perhaps in her mid to late sixties) with silver hair. Her feathered hat sported a large silver pin with a singularly set black onyx stone, and she had a matching silver and black onyx pendant that rode upon her huge, slightly overexposed, white bosom.

She went on, "I remember when you were just a little boy. You were just the cutest little thing." At this point, she gave me a great hug, placing her left arm around my right shoulder, and grabbing the back of my head with her other hand. I thought the woman was going to crush my face into her chest. I turned my head to the side and avoided suffocation.

Roberta continued talking about a great deal of things. She went on and on. "You know, I was just telling the neighbors the other day …."

Janet at last interjected, "Bertie, would you care for anything? Maybe a piece of pie?"

"Why, yes, I would. Tell me, is that your Aunt Denise's coconut cream pie?"

"Yes," Janet replied. "I made it myself last night."

"Well, in that case, I simply must have a piece. It's just to die for!!"

I remembered thinking, that if she ate enough of it, perhaps she would. I went to the table and brought back a decent sized slice with a fork. "Here you go," I said. "Enjoy."

Roberta took one bite of the pie and her face lit up. "Mmm, mm, mmm, mm, mm. That is just so yummy!" She turned to Janet, "You just have to give me that recipe!"

"Well, thank you! I'd be happy to get it for you," Janet offered.

"Don't trouble yourself right now, dear," Roberta said. "I'll stop by Sunday afternoon after church to pick it up. As I matter of fact, I'll just drop by here, since it's more convenient." She went on about the pie – "You know, the most important part about a pie is getting the crust just right. I've heard that it turns out best if you mix just the right amount of cold water with the ingredients, and of course you have to be careful not to bake it too long, or the crust gets too hard." Then she turned directly to me and announced, "I simply detest pie when the crust is hard. You know what I mean, don't you."

I assured her in no uncertain terms that I had no idea what she meant.

I don't think she heard me. She just went on talking. I found myself thinking that I wanted to pick up my shotgun and fire one blast over her head. Perhaps she would just run off. "Bye bye, Bertie," I thought. But she was still there, chattering away like some old crow. Her lips continued to move, but now I wasn't hearing anything she was saying – at least, it wasn't making any sense. I broke away, went to the punch bowl, and then spoke with a few other guests.

A bit later, I noticed Roberta over by the front window, alone. She appeared to be fussing with something on one of the side tables, but her back was toward me, and I could not see what she was doing. Perhaps she was arranging one of the doilies. No matter, it wasn't important. It just seemed odd that she was by herself, not talking with anyone. At that point, she turned and walked to the parlor to join some other guests.

Eventually, the guests started moving about the rooms as if they were caught up in a slow turning pool of water, circulating with each other in a small eddy about the parlor and the dining room. Then, like in the small vortex that forms when you pull the drain plug of a bathtub, they began to filter past Janet, expressing their appreciation and sympathy in what sounded like low, small gurgles. Then they gurgled their goodbyes to other guests, funneled out the front door, and flowed down the front walkway to their cars waiting at the curb.

The last three persons left in the rooms were Janet, me and Roberta. We were about to say goodbye when Roberta eyed the pie remaining on the serving table. "Would you mind terribly if I took a piece of that home with me? It's to die for!!"

I cut her another slice, put it on a plate and handed it to her. She must have noticed my watch. "Oh, my goodness," she exclaimed. "I must go right away!! I have to get to the bank before they close!" And then, "Don't forget, I'll be by Sunday afternoon to pick up the recipe." She said goodbye, hurried out the door to her car, and drove away.

*****

Once everyone had left, we changed into our everyday clothes and began cleaning up after the reception.

"Well, what do you think of Bertie?" Janet asked. "Don't you think she's nice?"

"Yes, nice," I replied. I thought I saw a little grin creep across my cousin's face. Then under my breath: "Thought she was about ready to move in."

"Jimmy? Did you say something?"

"Oh, no. Not really," I answered. "I mean, I was thinking what's the difference if they're made of lead and not tin?"

"What's made of lead?" Janet was busy adjusting the drapes in the parlor.

"Oh, never mind. It's not important."

We finished putting everything up. Janet washed the punch bowl and serving pieces, wrapped up the remaining sandwiches in two packages of tin foil (one for her and one for me), and put the leftovers in the refrigerator. I took the trash out and came back inside.

"I really didn't get a chance to say this earlier," I began, "but I'm really sorry about your Dad. You have my sincerest sympathy."

"I know," Janet replied, "and thanks."

Then I shifted to a more jovial tone: "You really did a swell job with the reception, too. And that pie wasn't bad either."

She laughed. "Don't forget -- you promised to help me tomorrow. I'll call around nine before I come over?"

"That's fine," I said.

Then Janet turned quieter. "You know, I get the feeling there may be more to my dad's death. I mean, for some reason, I'm thinking he may have been murdered."

"Well, that seems kind of odd, don't you think? You said yourself that he died of a heart attack." Then I commented, "You've been reading too many mystery stories."

"Yeah, you're probably right." Then a pause. "Well, I'll see you tomorrow morning! Good bye, and thanks again for your help with the reception." She gathered up her things, walked out to her car and drove home.

6 SATURDAY
August 13, 1960

It was nine thirty when Janet knocked on the door. She had called about a half hour before, just as she had promised. I answered the door, all ready to go, but out of politeness asked her if she would like a cup of coffee before we left for her dads' place. She surprised me and said yes, so we went to the kitchen and had a quick cup.

"Do we need to get any cleaning supplies or trash bags?" I asked.

"No, there should be plenty of stuff at the house. Besides, if we need anything we can go over to the store. It's not far."

We left Aunt Dede's house, jumped in the car and started over to my Uncle Carl's place.

On the way, just out of curiosity, I asked Janet what caused her dad and his first wife, Ester, to separate.

"Well," Janet started, "It's kind of a long story. It didn't happen right away. To begin with, my mom was a biology student when she and dad married. Ever since he was a boy, my dad had a fear of spiders, but as time went on, it became worse. Ester naturally was interested in helping him get over his fears, so she wanted to learn more about insects and spiders. The more she learned, the more interested she became, so she eventually began studying entomology and then arachnology, and ended up getting an advanced degree. The problem was, the more she learned about spiders the more she wanted to talk about them, and this made my dad's problems even worse. The long and short of it is, she became fascinated with spiders, and he became more and more afraid. Even though she never brought any specimens to the house, it wasn't a good situation. He developed an absolute phobia, and started to dislike her as a result. She eventually received an offer for a teaching position at some college in California, and accepted it. That was the end."

I told her I was sorry that was how it all happened.

"That's okay. It's ancient history. My mom got over it after moving to California, and of course my dad remarried."

"Did he ever get over his fear of spiders?"

"No. He was absolutely terrified of them."

*****

Janet parked her car in the driveway leading to her dad's garage. She went up the side steps and unlocked the door to the kitchen. Like Dede's place, the house was built off grade, so there was no basement. Janet explained that her parents (Uncle Carl and Ophelia) used the attic and the garage for storage. We looked around in a small closet off the kitchen, and found a stack of paper bags, and a few cleaning supplies. Janet wasn't sure exactly where to start, so I asked her what main rooms she needed to go through.

"Well, we probably need to get rid of dad's stuff in the bathroom, and we need to go through the bedroom to get rid of some clothing and maybe some other personal stuff. Then there's his desk, and stuff in the attic and the garage. I know it's not a big house, but it seems a bit overwhelming."

"Don't worry too much about it," I said. "We just need to start with one room at a time. Is there anything you know of that you want to keep? I mean, personally?"

Janet mentioned that she would keep some of her dad's jewelry (rings or a watch), maybe some books, or items of sentimental value, but nothing too personal such as clothing. I suggested that as we go through each room, we put stuff in three groups—one to keep or sell later, one to throw out, and one to donate. She seemed to think this was a good idea, so we took the supplies up to the bathroom, and started going through things. She decided to throw away pretty much everything we came across that belonged to her dad (deodorant, shave cream and such). The only exception was a Gillette double edge razor, which she decided to keep.

The next room we took on was the bedroom and the closet. She would donate all her dad's clothes in the closet. (It seemed funny to me that a person's clothes would still be hanging around, waiting to be worn, after the person had passed away.) The clothing in her dad's dresser (socks, underwear and pajamas) she decided to discard. There were a few personal items in and on the dresser that she kept – a watch, tie clips, and a couple rings. On the nightstand next to her dad's bedside was a Bible, which of course she kept for herself.

Opening the nightstand drawer, we noticed several other books that had been stuffed toward the back. There was a paperback novel entitled "The Black Widow" and a bunch of newspaper clippings about poisonous spiders. There were also a couple books or field guides devoted to spiders, with pictures and write ups on the various species. It seemed rather odd to us that a man terrified of spiders would keep such a collection in his nightstand.

"I'm not sure," said Janet, "but maybe he was trying to deal with his fears by reading about them." She left all the books and newspaper articles about spiders where they had been in the drawer.

*****

We carried the bags downstairs, and I took the items to be thrown out or donated to the garage. Meanwhile, Janet put the things she wanted to keep in her car. We then drove to a walk up hamburger stand for a late lunch, got a couple cheeseburgers and cokes, and ate in the car. Then we returned to her dad's house.

"What do you want to tackle next?" I asked.

"Oh, I don't know." Then she thought for a moment. "Let's take care of the attic this afternoon, and on Monday, we can finish up with my dad's desk in the front room, and with the garage."

I told her that was fine with me, so we went back upstairs. A fold-down ladder allowed access to the attic. Floor boards had been put in, so we could easily move around up there without having to watch where we stepped. Most of the stuff looked like it belonged to Ophelia. There were some small pieces of furniture – a couple of chairs and a stand up full-length mirror – and a trunk that was filled with her clothes. Several boxes of Christmas and Halloween decorations were also stored there. We didn't find much that belonged specifically to Carl. Then Janet spied one smaller cardboard box with Uncle Carl's name written on it. The box looked like it was recently opened, as the dust had been brushed off, and the cellophane tape securing it had been cut.

She opened the box and found a few more books about spiders, several rubber gag spiders, and a couple of wooden sticks with plastic spiders attached with long rubber bands.

"Gee, it looks like your dad really had a thing for spiders. It's almost like he was intrigued by them instead of being frightened of them."

"Yeah," Janet agreed, "it's really strange he would have so many books and things related to spiders. I mean, there's this stuff here in the attic and the things in his nightstand. It just doesn't make sense." Then she paused a moment, like she was deciding what to do. "You know, I'm going to take all this stuff with me."

So we took the box containing the spider things downstairs, and she put them all in her car.

We decided we had accomplished enough for one day. The next day was Sunday, a day of rest. We would finish getting Uncle Carl's stuff out of the house on Monday. My cousin then reminded me that Roberta Black would be coming over to Dede's house Sunday afternoon to pick up the coconut cream pie recipe, and that she (Janet) would call me ahead of time. Janet drove over to Dede's house, and dropped me off.

"See you tomorrow," I called out, as she started off toward home.

7 THE RECIPE
Sunday August 14, 1960

I awoke at nine thirty, well rested and refreshed. It was my first really good night sleep since arriving in Jenson. My anxiety of the rail trip was now over, as was the anticipation associated with the reception – the preparation and having to meet strangers. I felt more relaxed, I supposed, because now I was involved in a concrete activity, helping my cousin with her dad's house.

I decided it was time for breakfast, and just to be adventurous, I took the back stairway. I entered the back bedroom, crept past the evil witch on the wall, and opened the door leading to the second floor landing. There was a light switch at the top of the stairs, so I did not have to descend in the dark. The staircase was narrow, and halfway down it reversed direction before ending on the first floor. I opened the door that led into the kitchen, and snapped off the switch at the bottom of the stairs. "A pretty nifty setup," I thought, "especially if you want to come downstairs without someone in the front rooms knowing about it."

There was about a half pot of coffee left over from Saturday, so instead of throwing it out, I reheated it in a small saucepan on the stove. It still tasted alright once I added a bit of milk and sugar. Besides, Janet and Roberta would be over in an hour or so, and I would make a fresh pot then. I fried a few strips of bacon and made some toast. Once breakfast was over, I cleaned up the kitchen and took the trash out. The only newspaper in the house was the Tribune I had bought at the general store Wednesday afternoon. I forgot to buy the early edition of the paper Saturday night, and since today was Sunday (a complete day of rest), the stores were all closed. "It's a good thing I'm stocked up on groceries," I thought.

The big thing to look forward to was Roberta Black coming over that afternoon to get her recipe. When I considered that prospect, and how uneventful Thursday was, I figured today would make Thursday seem like an absolute festival. At least breakfast was decent, and Janet would visit for a while. I went upstairs and straightened up the bedroom.

*****

It was about eleven thirty when Janet called and said she had been at church. She would be over in about an hour if that was okay. Roberta had told her that she planned on stopping by at one o'clock. I said that was fine, and reminded her to bring the recipe for the pie. I also asked her to bring the Sunday paper, if she was done with it.

"Yes, I'll put the recipe in my purse," Janet said. "And don't worry, I'll bring the paper with me. But I want to keep the sales flyers and the magazine and TV lineup sections. You know, I like to work the crosswords."

"That's fine," I told her. "I just need to catch up on the news, and to have something to read."

"Okay, see you in about an hour."

"Okay. Bye."

*****

Janet walked up to the front door and knocked. It was twelve thirty, and she was right on time. She stepped into the hallway, smiling as usual. It was nice to see her still in good spirits. Roberta arrived about ten minutes later. I asked them if they would like some coffee or anything.

"No thanks," Roberta replied. "I just dropped by to say hello for a minute, and to pick up the recipe for that pie." Then to my cousin: "You do have it, don't you, dear?"

"Oh, yes, of course. It's in my purse and I left it in the car. Please excuse me." Janet turned and went out the door.

In the meantime, I also excused myself and went upstairs for a minute, leaving Roberta alone in the dining room. When I returned downstairs, I used the stairway leading off the third bedroom and entered the kitchen at the back of the house. I could see Roberta through the entryway that connected the kitchen and the dining room. She was standing at the right side of the dining room window again, adjusting the doily while watching my cousin return up the front walkway. Roberta's back was turned toward me, and she was completely unaware I was watching her. Janet was still outside -- she had gone to her car to get her purse, but halfway back up the walkway had realized that she left the Sunday paper in the car. She had returned to the car, grabbed the newspaper, and was just returning to the house. Roberta walked to the front door and opened it.

Janet came in, gave Roberta a smile and placed her purse and the Sunday paper on the dining room table. She dug through her purse and found the recipe card. By this time, I had made my way into the dining room.

"Here you go, Bertie," Janet announced. "Now you can make the famous coconut cream pie too."

I couldn't help myself. "Now when you make the crust," I admonished in a sarcastic manner, "make sure you add just the right amount of cold water."

My comment must have been lost on Roberta. "To be sure," she replied. "And thank you, Janet, for the recipe. I'll make it for our next ladies' circle meeting. I'm sure everyone will just rave! Well, I must be going. Again, I'm so sorry about your father. He was such a wonderful man.

If there's anything I can do…. Well, goodbye." Then she turned to me: "So nice to see you again."

Janet and I both said goodbye to Roberta as she left. We watched in silence as she ambled down the sidewalk, climbed into her car and drove off.

I asked Janet again if she would like some coffee.

"Thank you, but not now. I need to get home soon. Oh, and I left the paper for you on the dining room table."

I told her thanks for remembering it, and also for coming over so I would not have to face Roberta alone.

"I can tell you don't like her, do you." Janet observed.

"It's not that. I'm just not that fond of her. She's a bit overbearing."

There was no response.

Then Janet reminded me that we would finish up at her dad's house on Monday. "Of course I'll call you before I come over. And thanks again, Jimmy, for helping me."

I told her to have a nice afternoon, and that I was happy to help out.

"See you tomorrow. Bye." And with that, Janet walked down the steps to her car.

I went to the kitchen, started up a fresh pot of coffee, and sat down to read the Sunday edition of the Tribune. There was an interesting piece about Model T Fords – "Song of the Tin Lizzie Splits Air as Hobbyists Hit Road". Then I turned to the comics section to catch up on Beetle Bailey and Dick Tracy.

8 DISCOVERY
Monday August 15, 1960

We arrived at Carl's house, and Janet opened the side door to the kitchen. The clock above the refrigerator showed it was about ten thirty.   We got a few more paper grocery bags from the small closet off the kitchen. I hadn't noticed them before, but today I saw a couple cans of insecticide on the floor in the corner of the closet. I read the label – Black Flag Insecticide -- Kills ants, roaches and spiders.

We decided to begin with Carl's desk in the front room. Janet didn't find much to throw out. Most of the items in the desk were either papers or office supplies that would remain in the desk. The same was true for the envelopes and postage stamps in the top drawer, as Ophelia would probably use these. Janet found her dad's pen and pencil set, a really nice set still in its case, and decided she would keep that for herself. She also kept a pair of brass elephant bookends that Aunt Dede had given Carl years before.

Once we were through with the desk, we went out to the garage. Janet got the keys to her dad's car, a 1956 green and white Chevy Nomad station wagon. It would come in handy to haul the bags to the donation center. Uncle Carl's tools were stored either on his workbench, or hung on the garage wall above it. Janet would leave all the tools and the lawn tools and equipment in the garage. Ophelia could use them later, or they could sell them. Again, I noticed several cans of Black Flag - this time on the garage floor next to the workbench. There was also a small stack of newspapers and magazines that was set on top a box of Mason jars in a corner of the garage. When we picked up the stack of papers to throw them out, we found that most of the jars had their lids screwed on, and there were several small holes punched in the center of each lid. Janet picked up the jars and examined them closely. In the bottom of four or five of the jars were dead spiders of varying sizes, their little black or brown bodies all crumpled up -- well, like dead bugs.

"Creepy," she exclaimed.

"It sure is. It's like your dad was collecting them."

"Yeah. Or someone else was," she said pensively.

We left the box of Mason jars where it was. Janet would wash them all out later. I started to load up the station wagon with the bags of stuff to be donated. There were more cans of insect spray in the car - one in the cargo area and one on the floor board of the back seat. I put them in a bag to throw out. Once we got the station wagon loaded up, Janet decided to check the bedroom once again. She found a flashlight in the kitchen, and we went upstairs.

"I forgot to check under the bed the other day," she explained. "And besides, I want to get those books and clippings out of his nightstand." She put the items from the nightstand drawer in a small box, and I took the flashlight, got down on my stomach, and looked under the bed. There was nothing stored under the bed, but that didn't mean there wasn't anything to be found.

"Janet," I called, "take a look at this!"

I pointed the flashlight toward the corners of the bed frame where it met the headboard and footboard. There must have been at least a dozen spiders in their webs in the corners.

"Holy Toledo," she cried. "Quick, get the bug spray!"

I rushed around the house and got a can of spray, came back upstairs and doused each web with a deluge of insecticide. "Well, if that doesn't kill them," I observed, "nothing will."

I took the flashlight and double checked to make sure the spiders were in fact all dead. "Deader that a door nail," I announced. I swept them all up with a brush and dustpan and deposited them in a trash bag, making sure to destroy all the webs and any egg sacks. Then I brushed off my hair and my shirt, making sure I hadn't picked up any stray hitchhikers.

Janet wondered aloud, "I just can't imagine why there would be so many spiders under the bed."

"I'm not sure," I replied. "Maybe your dad started collecting them, and they just got out of hand. You know, some type of infestation, or something. Based on the number of spray cans I've found, it definitely looks like he was trying to control them."

At that point, I noticed there was a small section of flooring near the edge of the bed that was loose. I managed to pry the loose board from its position with one hand while holding the flashlight with the other. I moved the board to the side, and in an instant, a large spider charged toward me from the cavity in the floor. It stopped just short of the edge of its hole, which was lined with a network of thickly interwoven webs. There was a huge brown fuzzed head with four sets of black eyes and two large yellow fangs. I immediately slammed the board down on the opening, and grabbed the spray can. I again lifted the board, and emptied the entire contents of the can. I waited for about a minute. There was no further sign of the spider. I was certain I had killed it. No further signs. I mustered up my courage and peered into the hole in the floor. Janet handed me a screwdriver, and I cleared out the webbing from the spider's nest. There, at the bottom of the opening was the dead spider. I took the blade of the screwdriver and crushed its huge body. Only then did I replace the loose floor board.

I told Janet that I had enough of spiders for the day, and I think she understood why.

We were about to leave to go downstairs when Janet noticed a couple things on Ophelia's dresser that looked out of place. There was a small dark blue book. On closer examination, it proved to be a savings account passbook, with "First Jensonian National Bank" inscribed in silver letters on the cover. Janet opened the passbook, thumbed through it and read the last entry. Fifty-five thousand dollars had been withdrawn from the account on the first of August. That was a Monday and four days after Carl had died. The other item that seemed out of place was a singular piece of jewelry that had been left out. It was an obsidian pendant, jet black with an etched outline of a white spider. Janet recognized it as belonging to her mother, although she rarely saw her wear it. It was indeed a strange piece of jewelry. Oddly, it had been left in the open and not placed with the other items in Ophelia's jewelry box. Janet picked up the necklace and was about to place it in the jewelry box in the dresser, when she found that the box was totally empty.

"That's strange," noted Janet. Then after a moment: "She probably put all her jewelry in the safe deposit box at the bank. So I guess it's not so strange after all. But why would she leave this one piece out on her dresser?"

"Maybe she was getting ready to leave on her trip, and didn't have time to go back to the bank just to put this one last item in the safe deposit box," I suggested.

"I guess that makes sense." Janet then picked up the small cardboard box with the books and clippings, and we headed back down the stairs. She put the box in her car, along with the other box from the attic.

*****

Janet handed me the keys to the station wagon. "You can drive, if you want."

The Chevy started up after one or two cranks, and I glanced at the fuel gauge. "We can use some gas," I observed. "It's about half empty. I'll buy."

"Okay," she answered, "If you want to. There's a gas station on the corner near the donation center. I'll show you where."

She navigated while I drove. We pulled into a Standard Oil station, rolling over one of the rubber hoses stretched across the driveway entrance. The bell inside the service station sounded - Ding, Ding - announcing our arrival. I pulled up to one of the pumps and glanced at the price of regular gas – Thirty-two point nine. "A bit high," I thought to myself. The service attendant came out and crossed over to us. "Can I help you?" he asked.

I put on my role of typical gas station customer: "Yeah. Fill'er up, Mack. Regular."

The attendant was dressed in a blue uniform with a blue cap. There was an embroidered patch on his shirt: Standard Oil. A professional looking uniform, I thought. A lot better than having some gas jockey in a white Tee shirt with a pack of Lucky Strikes rolled up in his sleeve and a chip on his shoulder.

He opened the car's gas cap, and started the pump. Then he came over to my window. "Check the oil?" he asked.

"Yeah, and can you look at the battery?"

He inspected the oil and battery levels, then closed the hood. "Everything's good under the hood," he declared in sing-song.

Then he proceeded to clean the windshield, and in the meantime, the gas pump had cut off. He finished the windshield, went over to the pump, and squeezed the last few cents of gasoline into the tank. He replaced the gas cap and completed the fueling operation, shutting off the pump. "That'll be three dollars and eighty."

I gave him four dollars. "You keep the change."

"Thank you, sir," he responded. "And thanks for choosing Standard."

I started up the car. I said he was welcome, and told him goodbye: "See ya later, alligator."

I turned on to the main road, and Janet guided me to the donation center.

*****

After dropping off the bags of household items at the donation center, we drove to the Main Street Diner for a late lunch. Janet ordered a Pepsi with a grilled cheese sandwich deluxe, and I got a bowl of chili and a Pepsi. She insisted on paying for lunch, so I took care of the tip. Then she brought up the topic of Ophelia withdrawing the money from her savings account.

"How much did you say was withdrawn?" I asked.

"Ophelia took out fifty-five thousand. That's enough to live on very comfortably for five or six years. Why would she withdraw so much money just before going on a trip to Jamaica?"

"Well," I tried to explain, "she would need some money to cover final expenses, and then there's the money she would need for the trip. Maybe she was planning on buying a new car?"

"That wouldn't require fifty-five thousand. I mean, that's a lot of money! The cremation, service and all, would probably be two to three thousand at the most, and the trip won't cost more than two thousand, total. Even if she bought a brand new car, I mean a really nice one, that shouldn't be more than five thousand. That's a total of about ten thousand, maximum."

"Maybe she took it all, and skipped the country." I was halfway joking, and halfway serious.

"That doesn't make any sense either. Otherwise, she would have taken all the money out of the account."

"You mean there's more left?" I asked in disbelief.

"Yes, quite a bit more." And then: "Are you crazy? She wouldn't just leave the country permanently! She probably put the money in the safety deposit box along with her jewelry. You know, people do strange things when they're under stress."

I told Janet she was probably right.

We left the diner and started heading back to her dad's place. We would have to take all the trash out, since the next day was Tuesday – trash day. I was driving back down the main street, and we passed the Bijou Theatre where Psycho, Alfred Hitchcock's latest movie was playing.

"Hey Janet," I started, "What do they call the candy they sell at the Bijou?"

"I don't know. What do they call it?"

"Bijou Jou-Bi's," I quipped.

"Ha, ha, ha," she said. "Where do you come up with these things?"

Then I asked her, "Have you seen Psycho, yet? They say it's a real suspenseful thriller, one of Hitchcock's best. It stars Anthony Perkins and Janet Leigh."

"No," she replied, "and I won't go to see it. Those types of movies scare me to death."

"Are you sure you haven't seen it?" I joked.

Just then a white Ford sedan pulled right out in front of us. I slammed on the brakes, turned the wheel and just barely missed it. The Ford kept going down the street. "Screwball driver," I yelled. "He ran right through the stop sign." Then to Janet, "Are you alright?"

"Yes. I'm okay. Just a bit rattled. That was a close one, but nobody's hurt."

*****

We had narrowly avoided "Customization by Crunch," and managed to get back to Carl's in one piece. I parked the car in the garage, and Janet helped me get all the items to be discarded out of the garage and to the curb. Then she dropped me back at Dede's place on her way home.

She reminded me the garbage men would also be coming to Dede's neighborhood, and to be sure to take out the trash can. Then she asked me, "Jimmy, when do think you will be going back home? I mean, I appreciate all your help and everything, but I know you have to go back sooner or later."

"I expect to leave probably by Friday. That will give me two days for travel, and Sunday for resting up before I return to work. That reminds me, I'm starting to run low on groceries. Could you take me over to the store tomorrow, so I can get a few things?"

"Sure," she replied. "Just give me a call in the morning, and I can come by to pick you up."

"Okay, thanks."

She drove off. I went to the back of Dede's house and entered the kitchen through the utility area. I made sure all the trash was picked up from the bathrooms and kitchen, got the trash can from out back, and put it out at the curb.

*****

I woke up in the middle of the night and checked my watch: Three thirty. That meant it was two thirty central time. I was having a bad dream, but it didn't make any sense. I was being chased by enormous spiders with eight black eyes and yellow fangs. Then a large crow kept swooping down trying to peck at me. There was a black queen, and for some reason, Anthony Perkins and Alfred Hitchcock were trying to murder me. Then suddenly a light had come on and I awoke, but I couldn't recollect my thoughts. I tried to remember, but I couldn't.

I went back to sleep.

9 SUSPICION
Tuesday August 16, 1960

I already had lunch and was sitting in the parlor, waiting for Janet to drive up to the house. I had called her around ten thirty that morning and asked her to pick me up shortly after twelve. It was about twelve fifteen when Janet's car appeared outside the window. Before she could get out of her car, I had emerged from the front door and was walking toward the sidewalk.

I asked her if she ate lunch, and she said yes, and that she was fine.

"Well, are you ready to go to the store now?" I asked.

"Sure," she said. "You're in a bit of a hurry today, aren't you?"

"Not really," I responded, "I just wanted to get started."

"Okay, then. Let's go."

I got in the car, and she gave me a smile. She put the little car in gear and we took off toward the general store.

We arrived at the store in less than ten minutes. She parked the car out front, and we walked in. Our cousin Carolyn, one of Uncle Dennis' daughters, was working the store that day. She came right over to us, and asked how we were doing. We said we just came over to buy a few things, and that we were very glad to see her again.

"It was really nice of you, Janet, to invite me, and of course Denise and Dennis, to the reception on Friday. We all were glad to stop by to see you. Everything was so nicely done, you really must have put a lot of effort into it for your dad and all. It really showed. And Jimmy, it was so nice to see you again. It was really very kind that you came all the way from New York, and we so enjoyed visiting with you. It must be almost seven years since we've seen you last."

We both thanked Carolyn for the nice things she said, and for coming to the reception for Carl.

Carolyn then asked, "Jimmy, how long do you plan to stay in town before you head back home?"

"Well," I started, "I was planning on staying most of this week, and will probably leave on Friday." Then I asked, "Do you know if I need to buy my train tickets in advance?"

"Oh, heavens no!" she replied. "You just need to show up at the station about a half hour before the train leaves. You can buy your ticket anytime you're ready. The train pulls out of the station each morning around ten thirty for Chicago."

"Well good. That gives me some flexibility, in case I need it."

"So … You said you came in to buy a few things? Is there anything I can help you with?" Carolyn asked.

"Yes, I came over to get groceries and some other stuff. I think we can find it all, but thanks for asking."

Janet and I went about the store, collecting the items on my shopping list: A quart bottle of milk, some lunch meat and cheese, and a six pack of Budweiser. I still had enough bread, eggs, bacon and coffee to last through the week. I also remembered to get a newspaper and some cans of insecticide to replenish the supply at Carl's house.

We proceeded to the cash register. "Is there anything else?" Carolyn asked.

"No," I said, "That should pretty much do it."

Carolyn rang up the total, and I paid her.

"Thank you. See ya again later," she shouted after us.

"Bye for now." And we went out to the car.

We got in, and headed for Dede's place.

*****

After we had put all the groceries away, I plugged in the percolator and made a pot of coffee.

I decided to tell Janet about my dream. I told her about being chased by the spiders with their black eyes and large yellow fangs, and how the crow was trying to swoop down at me. I told about the black queen and how Alfred Hitchcock and Anthony Perkins were trying to kill me, and how I suddenly awoke but couldn't remember what I was supposed to remember.

The first thing out of her mouth was, "What on earth did you eat before you went to bed?"

"I don't know what made me dream it, but imagine being chased by Alfred Hitchcock!"

We both had a good laugh.

Janet started, "Well, no matter what, I just can't bring myself to watch a horror film like Psycho. Those kinds of movies scare me to death."

Then the light bulb came back on.

"Do you know what I'm thinking?" Janet asked.

"Yes," I replied. "Ophelia murdered your dad."

"Exactly." Then a short pause. "Only he died of a heart attack."

"Exactly," I continued. "He was terrified of spiders, and she must have used them to frighten him to death. I mean, look at what we found at the house. Spiders all over the place – in the garage in those mason jars, under the bed and in that cavity under the floor board. Then there was that box of stuff up in the attic, and all the books and newspaper clippings in the nightstand. And we found a half dozen or so cans of insect spray in the kitchen, the garage and even in his car. And to top it all off, she left her calling card out in the open – that black cabochon with the white spider design, After he died, she rushed the cremation service, withdrew a large sum of money, probably took all her jewelry with her and fled to Jamaica."

"I don't know," Janet said doubtfully. It seems a bit far-fetched. It's not likely that Ophelia would actually murder my dad. Yes, they were having problems, but she didn't seem to hate him or want to kill him. Besides, what you are talking about is just circumstantial evidence. There's no way to prove anything. Besides, if she did flee the country, why would she leave all that money still in her bank account? And it's unlikely she would purposely leave that one piece of jewelry out, since anyone could easily put all the pieces together and then suspect her. No there needs to be another explanation. Maybe my dad just died of a normal everyday run-of-the-mill heart attack."

"It just looks suspicious to me," I observed. "But perhaps you're right. They say the most obvious explanation is often the correct one."

"Well, it's easy enough to find out what happened to the money and the jewelry," Janet stated. "All we have to do is go to the bank tomorrow and look in the safe deposit box."

"What about the police? Do you think we should contact them?" I asked.

"I don't think so, at least not yet. Let's first find out what's in the box at the bank. I'm glad I kept all that spider stuff – it's still in boxes in my car. And I didn't wash out those dead spiders from the Mason jars – all that is still in the garage, just as we found it."

"Since we aren't going to the police just yet, maybe I should take the time this evening and start documenting all the facts as we know them so far," I offered. "That may help us in our thinking and help guide our investigation."

"Yeah. That's probably a good idea. We'll go to the bank tomorrow and maybe find out a little bit more. Then we can decide whether to involve the police. What do you think?"

I told her that sounded like a good plan.

 So that evening, after Janet had gone home, I began putting the wheels in motion.

10 THE TELEGRAM
Wednesday August 17, 1960

Janet came over about ten. I offered her some coffee that was still hot from breakfast and asked if she would like some of the sandwiches from Friday's reception (I assured her that they were still somewhat fresh).

"Just some coffee, thanks."

I poured her a cup and one for myself, also. "Here's what I've put together so far," I started. "I tried to jot down just the facts as we know them. Once we get those straight, we can determine who would or would not be involved based on motive, opportunity, and the means to commit the crime. See what you think."

"First the facts." (I must have sounded like Joe Friday on Dragnet.) "Your dad died of a heart attack at his home on July twenty-eighth. Then, four days later, Ophelia withdrew fifty-five thousand dollars from her savings account - Monday August first."

"Wait a minute," Janet interjected, "We don't know it was Ophelia who made the withdrawal. We just know the money was withdrawn."

"Okay," I conceded, "But we did find the bank passbook on her dresser."

"Well," Janet said, "It's easy enough to find out who made the withdrawal. All we have to do is check at the bank."

I continued, "Then on August second, Ophelia left on her trip. You said she was going to some Caribbean island – most likely Jamaica."

"Yes, that is what she said," Janet confirmed. "She wanted to get away, with all the stress and all." Then after a moment, "Don't forget to jot down that my dad was cremated on Saturday July thirtieth."

"That's a good point." I took a minute to make a note.

"Are there any other facts, other than hard evidence, that we know of?" I asked.

"We know dad was terrified of spiders," Janet observed.

"Yes. Who knew that?"

"Pretty much everyone," Janet said. "Me, Ophelia, Ester, the neighbors …"

"Well we know you didn't kill him, and Ester is in California. So the only people who had the opportunity to harm him, if our theory is true, are Ophelia and the neighbors. But I guess we are getting ahead of ourselves."

Then I went on, "In terms of evidence, this is what we found at your dad's house: Field guides of spiders, a paperback book entitled "The Black Widow" and several newspaper clippings relating to poisonous spiders, all in his nightstand drawer; In the attic we found a cardboard box that apparently had been recently opened and that contained some more books about spiders, rubber gag spiders, and spider toys; six cans of insecticide, two each in the garage, the broom closet, and in his car; numerous dead spiders in the bottom of Mason jars, with the lids screwed on – these in the garage; there were a dozen or so spiders in their webs under his bed, and one very large hairy spider in a cavity under a floorboard near the edge of the bed."

Then I asked Janet, "What else did we find?"

She responded, "Well, we did not find any jewelry in Ophelia's jewelry box. The only piece of jewelry we found was that pendant with the spider outline that was left out on her dresser. We also found the bank passbook also left out on her dresser."

"Is that it?" I asked.

"Yes, I think so. Except Ophelia mentioned she wanted all Carl's stuff gone from the house by the time she got back from her trip."

"That's probably a good point to jot down," I said, and I made a note of it. "What other evidence do we need to gather or clarify?"

"Well, we need to go to the bank to check on three things," observed Janet. "We need to see who withdrew the fifty-five thousand from the savings account. Then we need to check the safe deposit box to see if all her jewelry is there and likewise to see if the money that was withdrawn is there."

"Okay," I asked, "Based on what we know so far, who had the motive, the opportunity and the means to commit the murder, if in fact it is a murder?"

"Ophelia," Janet reluctantly replied.

"Is there anyone else?"

"No one that I can tell at this point," she said.

I was able to persuade Janet to have a couple of the small sandwiches and a glass of soda for a light brunch. After eating, we left for Carl's to pick up the bank passbook. From there, we would go to the bank.

*****

We were about ready to leave for the bank. Janet had just retrieved the passbook from Ophelia's dresser, and we were about to go out the side door to the driveway where the car was parked.

There was a knock at the front door. "Western Union," the voice at the door called.

We went to the front door and Janet opened it. There on the porch was a young man, probably eighteen to twenty years of age, wearing a drab-brown military style jacket.

He had a matching color service style cap, and Western Union Insignia were on both his cap and over his jacket pocket. His dull brown-painted bicycle was parked on the sidewalk.

"Telegram for Miss Janet Kelly," he announced. "Please sign here."

Janet obliged by signing some paper on his clipboard.

He handed her a light-brown sealed paper envelope. She handed him a quarter. "Thank you, ma'am," he said, and turned and walked toward his bicycle.

Janet closed the door, walked over toward the couch, and opened the envelope. "It's from Kingston, Jamaica." She glanced at it briefly, turned pale, and then collapsed onto the sofa.

"Janet," I exclaimed, "What is it? Are you okay?"

She just reached out with one arm and handed the telegram to me. It read as follows:

WESTERN UNION
Telegram

Origin: Kingston, Jamaica
Date & Time: 17 Aug 60   08:12
OPHELIA DEAD   STOP
BITTEN BY POISONOUS SPIDER   STOP

I didn't know what to think or do. Finally, I asked Janet if she wanted a glass of water or a hot cup of tea.

"Both," she replied, weakly.

I went to the kitchen, found a glass, and poured some ice water for her. I brought it out to her, and she started taking some sips. Then I went back to the kitchen and made us both a cup of tea.

In about fifteen minutes, the shock started wearing off, and she began to function as normal. The combination of the ice water and then the tea was working.

Finally she asked me, "What do you think? I mean, about Ophelia and everything?"

"I'll tell you what I think. I think she did it. No doubt. Only this is poetic justice if I've ever seen it! Plotting to kill her husband by scaring him to death with spiders all over the house, and even under his bed! The poor guy passed away from a heart attack, alright – all nice and neat. No murder weapon, and no poison. He appears to die of natural causes, and she gets off without a hint of suspicion. Then she goes off immediately to a vacation paradise and gets bitten by a spider and dies. You know, in the Bible, it says those who live by the sword shall die by the sword. So there you go."

After a minute of silence, Janet spoke, "I know you think Ophelia did it, and I can see why. But I don't know. Something just doesn't seem quite right, but I can't put my finger on it."

I began, "I know this must be a big shock. It is for me, too. Why don't you just try to take it easy and relax this afternoon?"

"Well, I guess there's no rush now to go to the bank. But I still want to find out about the withdrawal and what's in the safe deposit box."

"We can do that tomorrow, if you're feeling okay by then," I suggested. "You probably just need to rest up this afternoon."

She agreed, and I fixed a more substantial lunch for us. After a while, she started to feel much better. She wanted to go home, and she said she felt good enough to drive without any problems. I reminded her to make sure she had the passbook for tomorrow. She doubled checked, and made sure both the passbook and the telegram were in her purse.

She then took me over to Dede's, and from there she drove on to her place.

I took advantage of the afternoon to update the list of facts we had been documenting. There was no longer a need for us to rush the investigation – according to the telegram, our suspect was now deceased.

11 BLACK QUEEN
Thursday August 18, 1960

We were once again getting ready to head over to the bank. It was now about ten thirty. Janet had come to pick me up at Dede's place about a half hour earlier, but it was one of those mornings when I just could not get ready on time. I fixed us both a small breakfast, rinsed the dishes, and left them in the sink to soak. I would wash them later.

I made sure she had the little blue bank passbook in her purse, and asked her about the safe deposit box key.

"Yes, I have the passbook here with me. Wait a minute. I must have left the deposit box key at home. No matter, there might be one right here at Dede's." She explained that her mom and dad always kept a spare key with Aunt Dede.

Janet went over to the table lamp on the right side of the dining room window. She tipped the small lamp to one side. Covering the bottom of the lamp base was a round sheet of brown felt with a crossed double slit in the center. She reached into the opening with her index finger and extracted the small flat key. She returned the lamp to its position on the table, and straightened the doily. "There," she said, "Just as I expected."

Another light bulb flickered. "Janet," I said, "When we get to the bank, don't be too surprised if there's something missing from the safe deposit box. I'll explain it later."

She gave me a puzzled look and shrugged her shoulders.

I excused myself and went upstairs for a moment to get my wallet. Just as I came down the staircase into the parlor, the phone rang and I answered it. It was Roberta – there was no mistaking her booming voice, even over the phone.

"Hello, Jimmy? Is your cousin there?"

"One minute." I put my hand over the phone's mouthpiece, and announced to Janet, "It's Roberta. She wants to speak to you."

Janet came to the phone, said hello, and then started listening to Roberta. Bertie could have been on a megaphone instead of the telephone. I heard every word of the conversation just as if she were standing in the room with us: "Sorry, dear. I just heard the news about Ophelia. I know exactly how you must feel …" (on and on) … "Ophelia …" (on and on) … "Poor dear …" (on and on) … "And so far away from home …" (on and on) … "Let me know if there's anything I can do …. Now, you don't hesitate to call …"

Then she spoke of the coconut cream pie: "And thank you, dear, for that wonderful recipe … I just can't wait to make that pie. It's just simply to die for …"

Then: "You know, I just read the most interesting book. It was all about poisoned spiders, and that sometimes some people get so scared of them that they actually …" She stopped in mid-sentence. Then quite abruptly, "Well, I must simply be going now. Something's come up. Talk to you later." Then she hung up.

Janet put down the phone. "Did you hear that?" she asked.

"How could I not hear it," I retorted.

We both sat down.

I began. "I believe we have our black widow."

"Well, not quite yet," said Janet, "But there's no question in my mind that she did it."

"I think we have plenty of proof so far, based upon what we know and what she said. How else would she know already about Ophelia's death?"

"It is a small town," observed Janet, "And news travels fast."

"I think it's time we went over to the bank. Depending on what we find, we should probably go to the police."

*****

The First Jensonian National Bank was just a few blocks up the street from Dede's house. Janet pulled the little coupe into the parking lot, we entered the bank and asked for the head teller. Yes, the teller was able to verify that it was indeed Ophelia who had withdrawn the fifty-five thousand from her and Carl's bank account.

We then went to the safety deposit box clerk's desk. The young man at the desk was pleasant and very helpful. He asked us for the box number and then retrieved the signature card for Carl and Ophelia's box. (Janet was one of the persons authorized to access the box.) A quick look at the signature card showed that Ophelia had accessed the box on the first of August. There was also another signature- this one on August twelfth, Friday – the day of the reception at Dede's house. It was hard to make out the signature, but the time of access was two forty-five. "Oh yes," the young man mentioned, "I remember the lady quite vividly. She rushed in here last Friday, all upset, thinking that the bank was going to close in fifteen minutes when we actually were going stay open for another hour or so. She was really strange, like she had just come from a party or something. She was an older woman with silver hair, all dressed up wearing a black shiny dress and a black feather hat. Quite odd, I must say."

Janet signed the signature card, and the clerk opened the vaulted area that housed the safety deposit boxes. We entered the small room, and the door locked securely behind us. Janet and the clerk both turned their keys in the locks, and Janet removed the box from its little compartment. The clerk excused himself from the area while we poured through the contents of the box. Besides several important papers (deeds, birth certificates, etc.), we found what appeared to be all of Ophelia's jewelry. We also found an envelope containing a large sum of cash. On the outside of the envelope, Ophelia had marked "Fifty-two Thousand." When we counted the cash inside the envelope, we found only seven thousand.

"Okay," Janet began, "All of Ophelia's jewelry is still here, so that must mean that she put it here for safe keeping while she was going on her trip."

"Yes," I said, "It appears so."

"What do you make of the cash?" Janet asked me.

"It looks like Ophelia took fifty-two thousand and left it in the box. She probably kept three thousand for her trip. Then, I would bet, Roberta came to the bank last Friday, and took all the remaining money out of the box, leaving just the seven thousand. Now, before we left the house today, remember how you got the key out from under that one lamp? Well, I saw Roberta fiddling with that lamp or the doily on Friday afternoon at the reception, and perhaps also on Sunday when she came to pick up the recipe. I didn't think anything of it at the time, but now I know she was getting the spare key and then returning it on Sunday. What do you think of that?"

"I think," Janet said deliberately, "We had better get hold of the police. After all, forty-five thousand dollars is grand larceny, and murder is murder."

*****

Once at the police station, we spoke with a homicide detective. We told him the entire story down to the last detail, and Janet presented the physical evidence she had at the time – the bank passbook, the telegram, and the objects from the nightstand and the box in the attic – all of which were in her car. The detective thanked us for coming in and providing such compelling and complete evidence. He promised to investigate further, and to keep us updated. He gave us his telephone number, in case we came across more information or had questions.

Then he warned us both not to speak to anyone – especially Roberta – about the case.

Lastly, he turned to me and asked if I planned to stay in town. I told him I had originally planned on leaving the next day to go back to New York.

"Don't," he admonished, "I will need you to stay here until we get this all wrapped up. Don't worry. It shouldn't take but a few more days."

12 CONFESSION
Friday August 19, 1960

The police arrested Roberta Black at the train station. She was about to purchase a ticket for the ten thirty train to Chicago when she was apprehended.

Janet received a call from the detective and we were asked to come down to the police station that afternoon as he wanted to inform us of the progress in the case. Upon our arrival, I glanced at the clock in the detective's office. The time was two fifteen. Detective Johnson began by saying Roberta had been apprehended earlier and was in police custody. At the time she was arrested, she had ten thousand dollars with her, and had already transferred thirty-five thousand by wire to a bank in Philadelphia. (The wire transfer is what tipped the police off that she was about to leave town). Detective Johnson also went on to say that they had investigated with the authorities in Kingston Jamaica, and sadly, the telegram was authentic. Ophelia had indeed been bitten by a poisonous spider and died. Apparently, the spiders had been planted in her suitcase, and Ophelia was bitten as she slept.

Janet asked, "How did Roberta react when she was arrested?"

"She was at first absolutely shocked that she had been stopped by our men. I think she was mostly embarrassed being arrested by the police in a public place such as the train station, and then being brought here in a patrol car. After she got here, she was read her Miranda rights, and I think that almost scared her to death, especially the part about 'anything you say can and will be used as evidence against you in a court of law.' It's safe to say, she did not react very well. Of course, no one likes being arrested."

"Think of her poor family." Janet sympathized, "Her sister and niece still live here in Jenson. They'll just be devastated when they hear the news."

"Yeah," I added in my sarcastic manner, "Just think of the scandal!! I guess she's really given her family a black eye!"

Janet tried to ignore my comments.

Detective Johnson continued: "Roberta was offered the opportunity to secure an attorney, but she declined."

The detective went on to explain the details of what happened next.

To sum up what Detective Johnson told us, Roberta was presented with the facts and evidence and the police brought some pressure to bear.

After an hour of questioning, she cracked like an egg, and then started singing like a bird. Only the song she sang wasn't quite the tune we expected.

She admitted to placing the poisonous spiders in the suitcase thereby killing Ophelia. She also admitted to stealing the forty-five thousand dollars. She did not however kill Carl, at least not directly. Instead, she put Ophelia up to it. Ophelia was the one who scared Carl to death by planting those spiders in the house. So in the end, Roberta persuaded Ophelia to commit the murder. They plotted it together. Roberta made the arrangements for Ophelia's trip to Jamaica, and when she got back, they would split the money fifty-fifty. But Roberta became greedy and tried to take over. She killed Ophelia with the poisonous spiders, and would have eventually fenced the jewelry and taken all the remaining money.

The police had taken it all down, word for word. Roberta had then signed the confession.

The detective asked us if we had any other questions regarding the case.

"No, not really," Janet answered.

"Well," Detective Johnson indicated, "Both of you are free to go. And thank you for your help in bringing this matter to our attention."

I told him that I would probably be going back to New York early the next week.

"That's fine," he said.

Janet mentioned that she might also take the opportunity to visit her mom in California for a short while.

I then asked the detective whether he felt Roberta would be tried and convicted.

"Oh, she'll be tried all right – probably on charges of grand larceny, wire fraud, conspiracy to commit murder, and second degree murder. You never know what a jury is going to decide, but with a signed confession, the charges should stick. My guess -- she's looking at ten to fifteen years."

"Guess she'll be a Jail Bird for a good long time," I added.

*****

On the way back to Dede's house, I asked Janet to stop at the general store, as I needed a few more things. We stopped in and I went to the back of the store. I got another quart bottle of milk, some more coffee, and a couple frozen TV dinners – the kind that come in the sectioned aluminum trays that you just pop in the oven. I found Janet on one of the aisles, perusing the crossword puzzle magazines.

"All set," she asked?

"Yeah, I'm ready to go back now."

At the cash register, we were met again by our cousin Carolyn. "You guys missed all the excitement this morning. That lady who was at the reception last week, Roberta Black, was arrested right across the street at the train station! They took her away in a police car and everything!"

"How awful!" Janet replied.

Carolyn went to change the subject. "So how are you doing? Been up to anything exciting?"

I quickly glanced at Janet and then spoke. "Haven't been up to much today," I confessed. "Maybe you'll read about it in the paper later."

Carolyn looked slightly confused, but rather than explain it all, we just said goodbye.

Janet still had a little grin on her face when we got to her car.

13 DEPARTURE
Monday August 22, 1960

I had already laundered my clothes and packed my suitcases over the weekend. On Sunday, I had cleaned the house, made sure the dishes were all put away, and then taken the trash out that evening. Janet had called and offered to take me to the station Monday morning.

She arrived at the house right around quarter till nine. We had a quick cup of coffee and I cleaned up the remaining dishes. I took my luggage out to her car, and the trash can out to the curb. Then I gave her back the key to Dede's house.

It was about nine thirty when we got in her car and left for the station. When I glanced at my watch, it showed ten thirty – there would be no need to reset it now. I remembered how Roberta had noticed my watch and then rushed off to the bank in a panic. I laughed about it, to myself, of course.

We arrived at the train station in just a few minutes. Janet parked the car, but did not immediately shut off the engine. I asked her to tell my other cousins goodbye for me, and to let them know when I had left to go back east. I thanked her for everything she had done while I was in Jenson.

"Jimmy," she said, "I ought to be thanking you. I mean, for helping me with the reception, and getting my dad's house cleaned out, and for all your help with the police and the investigation."

We were about to get out of the car, when she reached over and turned on the radio. This time it was Brenda Lee with her soft, smooth, Southern vocals. Janet turned down the volume a bit. The music was not too low, and it was still clearly audible. Brenda was finishing her song:

> *I'm sorry, so sorry,*
> *Please accept my apology.*
> *But love was blind,*
> *And I was too blind to see.*
> *(Sorry)*

Then Janet turned off the car's engine, and we went into the station house. I bought my ticket and checked my luggage. The enormous clock above the ticket window showed the time as nine fifty. I told Janet she did not have to wait for the train with me, but she nevertheless insisted. We sat down on one of the huge benches and passed the time. There were about ten or twelve other persons also waiting. About twenty-five minutes later, the train's horn and bell announced its arrival. One or two passengers got off the train, and we then got up and proceeded to the platform.

I told Janet goodbye again, told her to have a good trip when she went to California, and asked her to say hello to Ester for me.

"I will," she answered. "And take care of yourself, Jimmy."

I then climbed aboard the train, and settled into a seat next to a window facing the station. Janet was still there on the platform, waving goodbye as the train started off. I waived, and then watched her diminish with the station as the train gathered speed.

The train pulled onto the main line, and glided past the shops and factories on the north end of town. In a few minutes we would be crossing the Mississippi, then we would head east through the cornfields toward Chicago. Later we would again move on, toward home and the cynicism of the big eastern cities.

*****

About a year afterwards, I received a letter from Janet updating me on the outcome of Roberta's trial. Along with the letter, she sent several newspaper articles that explained the proceedings in more detail. Roberta had been convicted of all counts, and had been sentenced to twelve years in prison. Roberta's sister had passed away several months after the arrest (natural causes), and her niece, also a resident of Jenson, had moved away to Sioux City.

In her letter, Janet told me Ophelia had been cremated and her remains were left on some beach in Jamaica. On a happier note, all the stolen money had been recovered, and was returned to Janet. Also, Ester was planning on retiring from her professorship at USC and would be moving back to Jenson by the end of the year. Janet would move into Aunt Dede's house, and her mom would live at Carl's place again.

I refolded the letter and replaced it in the envelope. Janet had given me a small brass elephant from Dede's house that I now used as an ornamental paperweight. I put the envelope on my desk, and placed the brass elephant on top. The elephant, as I remembered, was supposed to bring good luck.

&&&&&

LITTLE MISS MUFFET

Little Miss Muffet
Sat on a tuffet,
Eating her curds and whey;
Along came a spider,
And sat down beside her,
And frightened Miss Muffet away.
-   Mother Goose

&&&&&

Little Jack Horner
Sat in the corner,
Humming a holiday tune.
Ere he finished his song,
A spider came 'long,
And Jack crushed the thing with his spoon!
-   Anonymous

ABOUT THE AUTHOR

Bruce Martin is a native of the Detroit Michigan area, and is a 1965 graduate of South Lake High. He holds a Master of Arts degree from Wayne State and a Bachelor's from the University of Michigan. A Vietnam Era veteran, he spent four years in the U.S. Navy, stationed aboard the USS Davis homeported in Newport, Rhode Island. He has since retired from the insurance industry, and resides in Northeast Florida with his wife and two of his three sons.

Crafted Web is Bruce's first published work.